MW01258709

novice

SEWANEE POETRY

Wyatt Prunty and Leigh Anne Couch, Series Editors

novice

poems

nida
sophasarun

LOUISIANA STATE UNIVERSITY PRESS   BATON ROUGE

Published by Louisiana State University Press
lsupress.org

LSU Press Paperback Original

DESIGNER: Michelle A. Neustrom
TYPEFACE: Arno Pro

Cover photograph courtesy Nida Sophasarun.

LIBRARY OF CONGRESS CATALOGING-IN-PUBLICATION DATA
Names: Sophasarun, Nida, author.
Title: Novice : poems / Nida Sophasarun.
Description: Baton Rouge : Louisiana State University Press, 2025. |
    Series: Sewanee Poetry
Identifiers: LCCN 2024047645 (print) | LCCN 2024047646 (ebook) |
    ISBN 978-0-8071-8390-8 (paperback) | ISBN 978-0-8071-8459-2 (epub) |
    ISBN 978-0-8071-8460-8 (pdf)
Subjects: LCGFT: Poetry.
Classification: LCC PS3619.O677 N68 2025 (print) | LCC PS3619.O677
    (ebook) | DDC 811/.6—dc23/eng/20241129
LC record available at https://lccn.loc.gov/2024047645
LC ebook record available at https://lccn.loc.gov/2024047646

for my parents
in memory

contents

Rainy Season

Cool Season

acknowledgments

I'm grateful to the editors of the following publications in which poems previously appeared, sometimes in different forms or with different titles: *32 Poems, Carolina Quarterly, ISLE, NELLE, New England Review, Porter House Review, Prairie Schooner, SWING,* and *wildness.*

I'm indebted to all the friendships spanning many seasons and continents. Thank you for the conversations that companioned me while writing: Abena Apau, Amanda Arnold, Jennifer Fumiko Cahill, Meagan Casselberry, Hannah Dufford, Jessica El Bechir, Kay Fillingham, Kristi Flis, the Gibsons, Danielle Gray, Daniel and Jacqui Groves, the HK Book Club, Sarah Hughes, Tom Hwei, Unhie Kim, Michelle Kwok, Clara Lambert, Tamara Lamuniere, Cindy Leung, the Lu-Warners, Anne Merwin, the Mezeys, Min Mitchell, Kristin Murray, Madisa Onni, Masumi Ono, the Parks, the Quinzios, Lea Rivera, Patricia Frechin Rodriguez, Colleen Sandick, Anasuya Sanyal, Josh Savitch, Jayne Schrantz, James Shea, Steen Simonsen, the Smith-Sweeneys, Judy So, Min Suh Son, Hillary Strasser, Amy Suardi, Dew Tiantawach, Alla Voronenko, Manar Waheed, Carl Watson, and my family at RUN Hong Kong (https://www.runhk.org/).

Deep gratitude to Leigh Anne Couch for selecting my manuscript and for reading so generously and thoroughly. To Wyatt Prunty of the Sewanee Poetry Series and the production team at LSU Press: Thank you for taking care of this book from start to finish.

I'm indebted to my first and best reader, Cecily Parks. Thank you for the years of steadfast sisterhood and reminders to submit. This book would not exist without you. Special thanks to friends who read my work in the past and became the voices in my head (in a good way): Jennifer Chang, Joseph Legaspi, and Jason Marak.

I'd like to thank all my teachers for their help and encouragement, with deep gratitude to Frank Bidart for his early mentorship. Special thanks also to Ricks Carson who provided the earliest nudges of support.

Thank you to all the people who looked after my son and mother, so I could write. Special thanks to Linda Eckenbrecht, Thanya and Varintra Ungbhakorn, and Samaisukh and Mod Sophasan for their familial support. Love and gratitude to Elissa Sorojsrisom for sisterhood.

Deepest gratitude to Joshua Huck, for all the love and encouragement over twenty-five years and seven countries. Thank you for our life together. Special love and thanks to Silas Sophasarun Huck, whose energy continues to change the game.

I'm most indebted to my parents, Manop Sophasarun and Kobkua Wattanaphan, who gave me everything they had, including a complicated communication style. And their forgiveness. This book is for them.

novice

Vassa Season

In this deluge, my wheels lose traction in a valley of mimosa

and orchid trees. Yet the monk wades through, unfazed,

as a plastic bag catches on his robes. He carries his bowl for alms.

The novices giggle and cluster. They accept—*bend,* they say—

and with each *vassa* season they grow another year older.

By this measure, I am zero.

My car stalls. It creaks and rocks from the current,

and I assess what I missed (crows flying low and ants

hauling larvae across my doorstep), as if I could prepare

for the next rain and be better at waking

from my soft-focus dream of the jungle and meet crisis

like an old, rowdy friend and expect certain violence

from the bone sky bearing down and the slurry of leaves

smearing the lines. So when I lay eyes on something

I buried, I may not die to see it

unearthed, shiny and snaking

around my legs. So I may drink

without drowning and live through something.

And be unafraid.

hot season

Southern Magnolia

I walk home barefoot from the pool.
The old, white neighbor takes his time,
and just as I pass the pink, foamy tide
of azaleas, he emerges from under
his oaks. He's kindly, or maybe just
polite. He mentions
the overgrown grass.
The old man thinks our family
is slovenly, cheap.
But he does the neighborly thing
and calls the house
to lend us some tools.
I pick up. He jokes, says he hopes
I wasn't waiting for a boy
to call. He says,
You're not like that, are you?

No, sir.
I'm 15. I give the phone to Dad.
I keep my head down at dinner, clean my plate.
Outside, the evening bruises.
The roux of dust and pressure
loosens. Fireflies appear. Raccoons,
then possums, shuffle up from the woods.
Every night, I climb the driveway
and smoke. I picture miles
of kudzu along the highway—
scales that flutter
as they take over.
Then I ash where the halo
of streetlight falls
half on asphalt, half on
the magnolia at the end
of the cul-de-sac, where we live,
and that tree lives,
older than the bees.

Violent Femmes

Summer, Atlanta, 1989, handstands
in your pool, and after Marco Polo
we rest elbows on the concrete lip
and ask each other what it means
to lose your teeth in dreams. At night
we play Contra and pluck carrot sticks
radiating from a bowl of ranch dip.
Skip to 13. We chug gatorade and gin
and you walk a straight line in the kitchen.
Outside I vomit in the daisy bed.
We churn out mixtapes and collages.
Wear corduroys, plaid flannel
and saddle shoes. Prank call. Boys enter.
I can't keep up and am mean too often.
New friends rotate in. Sleepovers end.
But we are loyal to some original feeling
and in April reach out for our birthdays
up to the last time on the phone ten years ago
when you are in LA and knitting. Trying to
"live in the moment," you chuckle low
and quip "hope this is it."
When you're gone, your dad returns some
of my old letters. It's your last prank where
instead of hearing your voice, I'm forced
to hear me, pretending not to need
anyone and worse, misusing curse words.
You'd laugh at the desperation.
Almost as desperate as our first meeting
on the playground swings: Strawberry blond
strands threading the chains, you toe the mulch
and ask, Have you even heard
of the Violent Femmes?
I lie and say Yes.

Teenagers at Night

One night I drove by Chastain Park in a Ford Squire belonging to the boy
with whom I was infatuated.

He laughed in the backseat, his arms around my best friend,
and ordered me to *drive anywhere.*

So I drove, for a moment giddy with privilege, the only route I knew
to and from school, until in the rearview I saw them tilting

out of the frame, and I had to veer—re-focus on staying, chastened, inside the lane.
I drove, wishing I didn't prefer the park in daylight for a child's game of tag,

so that perhaps I might be noticed by the imprint
my body made when it fell in the grass.

How I ogled others whose outlines invaded air—
when boundaries were ceded, someone gained a new empire.

That was the summer I rushed home to read *Jane Eyre.*
And I wrote in my diary things like: *Loyalty, until desire.* As if we had arcs
on *Dynasty.*

But that night, out from the watchful shadows of the baseball field
stepped a new friend
who was quiet and beautifully plain:

Rage—
who wanted for me this intersection
of poles and wires and grass at all corners

to be razed
so I wouldn't have to go on staring ahead anymore
waiting for the light to change.

The Paperback Room

We found them on a hunt for illuminated texts on the second floor of the library
in a quiet wing towards the back, a room with celadon green carpeting
and dark shelves—the paperback romances.
Windows lined one wall but we wouldn't have looked out the windows.
We sat and read aloud passages when we should've been writing papers.
We laughed at the tropes (she was klutzy and had no idea she was beautiful,
he was a cad who wanted to be a dad) but after "Her skin grew hot
with his gaze" we grew silent. In an almost holy way. We leaned against the shelves
and then eventually sprawled onto our stomachs completely focused
on reading to ourselves (the heat grew between her legs,
she came in mind-shattering waves, luckily she was on the pill).
Light faded and someone mentioned the dining hall closing
so we wrapped scarves, hauled on peacoats, and trudged up the hill
through broken-up and frozen-over floes of December snow.
In our warm, incandescent rooms we returned
to comparing Van Gogh's potatoes to Williams's plums.
Later my friend confessed she went alone to the paperback room the next day
and stunned herself with how she couldn't stop reading.
She was the most honest of us all about the chaos of her body,
and in that icy cloister of stone and bookish girls
I fell deeper for her (after all, the safest place is to be hidden,
but still to see) and her thirst for these objects
of obsession. Her study was not even as a bid for self-possession
but simply as a woman who plays with the wild deities
guarding dusty truths in the next room.

After Happy Hour

You laughed when he wasn't
funny, but you wanted him
to feel good. Unwrap your robe,
get in bed alone and know
the streetlight through the window
will play on your skin
and wake you in the night. Shift
further down. The pillow smells
like a girl (a guy once told you)
but it's just Pond's cold cream which
you use because your mom
believed it worked for her.
Close your eyes and imagine
instead the smell of wet
pavement—the hint
of alluvium and sweet
intimacy of worms as they drag
themselves across sidewalks
in the rain. Are they answering
a call, or are they
drowning? When they writhe,
is it need, or are they traveling
towards a light—
to the spaceship that is
coming or going. Could you
be the thin-skinned worm
in her stocking of organs
who received orders long ago
to twist out of earth
a newborn each time?
In the evenings, you try—
you head past the line
of cabs to a place you've
already been, and when
you get there, to
the men, conceal. Conceal
that you are alien.

Arles in March

On the train I saw my miscalculation:
the lavender fields were sage and gray.
Too early . . . still the mistral . . . stilted drip
of conversation until Bayonne
where we came upon a small boy
spinning cotton candy at a fair
and teenage girls lifting their chins
and twirling on stage in orange and green.
In their confidence I remembered us
as teens, so close we dipped our fingers
in the same pot of lip balm and smeared
them over our mouths as if flaunting
a secret. One dancer, though,
wore a burgundy lip
and it occurred to me later
that you and I had learned separately
how to line and fill in our lips—
all the control in the withholding—
as if trying on our mothers' afflictions
in pigment. So it was too late
by the time I took this photo of you
looking down at me through the axis
of the double helix staircase
in Chambord, where we crossed
over and under limestone floors
and emerged no longer each other's
witness. I thought our rending
would look more like the tearing apart
of one girl, but you are lit up
and getting lighter in a tunnel
of shell. The silence makes me think
I made up the whole thing. The trip
was my idea, but I have trouble
remembering Arles—the color
of the room where we stayed: a yellow
that needs translation.

Instagram Feed

I see you've been traveling

to places *shockingly beautiful and isolated*
with only *a handful of people* you *really love.*

Most have that hazy, ironic filter
and then a flare. But some

are crystal clear—maybe shot
from a peak, inside its thinning

atmosphere—.

I really love seeing your photos.

And now, after seeing these,
I'd love to see

some that didn't make it:

what those places look like,
where maybe the air is thicker—

closer to the shame
between bodies.

Or just a photo of you leaving and how you left it.

Some photos of the times you traveled
to that hour of night in your bed

where there are no clean lines
but rather a sticky impasto

as if you've been flying
through webs.

Where you're sardined with the bodies
of all your failures.

You could caption this one:
The capital city of your love

where on the outskirts
the sign states the miles you've driven

And yet *You Are Here*

in the night, stalling in the same
gasoline-drenched place

where your back is turned but I know your eyes
are open, and the hair around your temples

is wet, because your temples

are burning.

I'd love to see those photos

with some spin—some
breezy notes like,

Places that blew away
  when I pulled the pin.

Dear C—

Inauguration Day, 2017

You were lonely, lost. Under the gray and low-slung sky
we walked along the Neva to Akhmatova's house.
You pointed across the river to the fortress
that doubled as a prison and we stood
in front of the ashtray where Akhmatova
burned her poems.
You searched for a lover in Russia
based on your love for Anna Karenina
and I was tough on you for choosing how to love
based on a book we read
when we were nineteen.
I had no imagination.
Or rather, fear turned a coat hook
into a place to hang
yourself instead of a home
for the coat of someone returning.
But when have men who love each other
ever known safety anyway?
You found someone.
I wonder where you are and if you're watching.
There is no poem being read today.
All brotherhood is as strange
as that fortress across the water.
It's a lot to ask of you to remember
how we stood waiting
in the same air
as her ashen words. All her lovers
long gone, but then the silver
and green light filtered through
the birch trees outside her house—
delicate and penetrating as though
streaming through a church.

Come Back, Shane

At my grandparents' house, everyone is fed
something delicious. Father likes mangosteens,
and Mother craves guava. I eat coconut custard tarts.
My uncle eats at odd hours. He speaks loudly
and sometimes I catch him, glassy eyed and
smoking. We both have the same tapered fingers
and like to sing, but I sense, in his hunted gaze,
that while our family eats well, maybe we are also
in exile. He rarely goes out. Grandma and Grandpa
don't allow it. He names each shepherd mutt
Shane, after his favorite cowboy, so he can call out,
"Come back, Shane." Each pup is brought in
from the street and fed rice and liver. Each one
knows how to hunt for snakes and monitor
lizards. When one dies, another Shane is
taken. Grandpa built the house on a snake
swamp, and that's the curse of it. Mother and Uncle
are still there, and the fan's shadows are now ceiling
stains. The current Shane is a shiny-coated girl
who drops her chew toy at my son's feet. She plays
gentle but is chained to the jackfruit tree. When
another dog passes outside the gate, she goes berserk
and lunges at all who are not as well fed, and yet
they walk by, free and unashamed.

In the Parking Lot of 99 Ranch Market

From the car as a child I preferred to spy

on the lives of chins and torsos passing by

while my parents inspected

persimmons inside the market.

It was a break from being asked

equations. Also the market smelled

of anchovies and I wanted

lemons. I didn't know I wanted

things to be different. I just

wanted. Overhead the buzzards

circled the smudged sky. You can't leave

a child alone in the car anymore.

Now my cart squeaks through

the spicy fug of an Asian market

in another town where I pass

the fallen pyramid of lemons in search

of custardy, sweet persimmons,

but when I get home the ones I picked

give me cottonmouth. I missed

an equation. Now behind my kitchen sink

a smell, a passive-aggressive stink, grows

a bit like rotten milk—maybe a mouse

who got snapped up in the lure

of wanting a brownie

at the expense of the fruit chosen

for her. The buzzards circle.

A karmic fall. She did not pledge

allegiance and cannot

enjoy persimmon season now.

The Snake

Its neck is broken
but the rest is curious,

a cheek tilted up, mouth open
as if it were seeing

the pinched-off light
that was yesterday.

I killed it so we wouldn't
have to fear. But now fresh guilt

blossoms like the white gardenia
in the darkest green:

what had once sewn a deliberate
path—a seam in the grass, a vine's

gesture—now dangles, droops
de-threaded and crooked

from a thumb and knuckle.
A line without intention.

I misread the signs
of a beast coming in

from the rain. Now it's too late
to gaze up into the canopy

like girlfriends pondering
if we were desperate for change

or just afraid of life . . . if we were
always nervous or never.

Leaving Song

Orange dust coats the toes
walking this ruddy strip
of crumbling sidewalk
where I parse the beats
of moths in the betel
palms: this is your hair
falling, your voice slipping
in a kind of leaving
song. Now the fronds
blacken the rim of the lake
where we made plans
for when we would return
to the States. The note
that was your laugh—
I heard it last
over a shoulder midday
in hot season
walking to our cars and
hardly believing we wanted
the rain to start. The sound
plays tricks like the heat
wanting to stick.
For days then weeks
I heard you
in the bulbul's whistle
up in the yellow blossoms.

rainy season

The Forestry Minister's House

is abandoned. Hearts are cut into the window sill,
and there's not much else, except low, narrow beds.

Ghosts begin to populate: I see the daughter in her bedroom at dusk, maybe sick
from the switchbacks up the hill, or restless, overhearing her parents in the family
room.

She can't tell what is argument and what is small talk.
The voices are replaced by the radio, Sam Cooke singing

"Cupid," and she listens to him, instead of sleeping, and grows still.
I walk out through the porch into the field of pink crocuses and towering pines.

I pass the train station and wonder if I found my way back
because the track had already been laid down.

I left home, got married, moved around, and yet
there is no relief from form, from recognizing

the birth of a family's code, no matter how tangled
the morning glory grows. I follow the path

twisting through the blue trumpets until night
becomes a vista, and I step off this trail,

as if turning away will keep the land from welling up again.

Ants (in Four Acts)

i.

I spot a crack between the floor and baseboard
because a black ant crawls out.
Surprise and wonder—a mouth that widens
as the insides are eaten
by professional eaters
of dust and spilled things.

Did this breach come from my own feast?

ii.

I overate when I was young
because who doesn't?
I didn't know what to call it. It was a swollen gut.
Not my heart. I really was
sensitive.

None of this ended up being useful.

iii.

Mom always eyed me, who beckoned the ants—
those retrievers
of the sticky and soft. I would crush them
only to find double the next day.

It turns out each stamped body
still smells of food.

iv.

Mom is sick but doesn't cry about it.
The least I can do is give her that.

There is no dignity
in the clean-up.

But I see the dutiful ants,
how full they are

with just that. Still, I chase these feelings
and still it breaks my heart.

The Horses

At night I think about my mother—
how she no longer inhabits
all the rooms in her body.

I wonder if in her dreams
she walks outside or even flies
over the corrugated roof.

This fantasy feels like betrayal.

For she says she sleeps well—
so deeply she doesn't even dream.

But night comes, and
I send horses

to nod their way into her rooms.

They warm her halls and leave hair
in the hinges.

It's impossible for me to leave
her body alone.

She would be mad if she knew.

I've never been able to leave
an empty room

unpainted, which is the problem

with longing—

the horses take off

in the morning.

The Line

moves faster than

blood blooming

in water

yet I can't draw

fast enough an animal

who learns quickly

that sorrow

doesn't come

from stillness

but from water

folding back

on itself

The Hold

I ran up the hill behind the house with you, some steps behind me.

I thrilled in my slips in the dirt and tucking my chin, thought:

God, let the life inside me fall out, now among the aspens

whose leaves twist and strain like fish who struggle

because they are held.

When it spills out, I'll say: Yes, I knew it was too heavy to hold.

But then I reached the top, intact and without a plan.

Your hand caught mine, and the tight weave of day began

to shake itself loose. The beryl sky tumbled into evening's purple,

orange, and sage, and the earth billowed up into aster and lupine.

The moon was no longer our ground.

I stared out and you smiled as if you weren't also sad.

I wanted to walk beside you again in the tall grass—

to let all this breathing be a sound.

Doldrums

Every few years I watch this albatross

video. He waits, a glacier-white dab

bobbing in the South Pacific sometimes

for months. He addresses my dread.

He has been hunting for food as I do

for melodramatic things—his nape

as he dips into water is my mother's

bent neck as she cries and sorts laundry.

Or is it my father staring into the closet.

He tells me to go. How to find the house

when the oily density rearranges itself?

I watch the video: the bird must wait

to gain some momentum,

and the wind picks up eventually

and buffets his wings, which lift

into a *v*, then *m*, branding

the sun. He is almost stunned.

After the credits roll, I call a friend

and after years of what I've turned

into an unable-to-land joke

she softly says: Just call it what it is.

She's a Maniac

I thumb past a meme of Ben Affleck
(post-cry face tilted to the sky)
in a #mood, bowls of sensual
noodles, a 'gram of a pic of Holzer's
PROTECT ME FROM
WHAT I WANT and a still
of Roger Sterling from
Mad Men, subtitled: "You don't value
relationships." Now, do I like,
hide, or comment on a video
of a little boy dragging
an empty jug as he takes us on a tour
of a camp crowded with women
and children? The clip rewinds. The ground
is dry, and there are no men. It's happening
now. His sky is a dusty blue
robin's egg. He is the age
of my son, and I hover
until my thumb presses save
which sends it to a folder called
saved, where I also collected a gorilla
who spins to the track "She's
a Maniac" in a plastic blue kiddie
pool. She doesn't actually hear
the music; it's a track laid
over her. Sunlight streams in
through a square opening
as she spins in a vortex
and pounds the surface
to glitter, nebulizing the iron bars
and cinder blocks. I rewind,
complicit in returning her
to her cell since I like to watch
a dancer become the dance
as there is no saving ourselves.

Cherry Pits

Sofia, Bulgaria

I wait in the market
for the rain to pass
and watch a man smoke
a cigarette on a bench.
The rain pours a shawl
around the bullet
of his body.
Maybe he prays
or relaxes this way
so as to loosen
his neck from some
chokehold he mistook
for embrace.
The rain does not stop.
I step over the potholes
bobbing with cherry pits.
A sign warns: Do not
cherry pick. Still I see
the cashier's Guns
N' Roses tee, every day
three rows of dented
yogurt tubs, the slit
of butcher between
the curtain of hanging
pigs, and a constant reel
of models slinking towards me
on runways on cafe TVs.
And the man
who smokes in the rain
sighs as if he is
the rebar inside
concrete, trying
to stop himself
from becoming
the person he is.

Roses

Sarajevo, Bosnia

We drive past the stadium and the hill of tombs, and as the ground

flattens, old men fish in the river and two girls cycle along the banks,

their hair flapping in pale flags, and outside a dilapidated factory,

I recall the innkeeper describing her son and how he ran

to get water. She dragged a finger across the valley of her cupped

palm. Snipers shot him in the leg, which healed, but, she taps her

temple and trails off, staring out the door at the peach blossoms

dripping with rain. We drive further still from the mountains,

and it gets warmer, fewer bullet holes in houses, where babas sit

on plastic chairs in the twilight and watch children throw rocks

at our car. Their mouths are agape, maybe in a laugh or a shout.

They hate us or they're just being children. We drive

and get stopped for speeding. The police tell us to leave

and we are ashamed of some things, but most of all, to be

relieved. When the innkeeper woke from her trance she asked

if we had seen the mortar scars filled with red resin, "our roses,"

she called them, where they stopped running in the street.

Patience Is a Hunger, Too

Tidying the house,
I lift a block to find
a spider wrapping her arms
around a milky clutch.
I ask her: Do I exist
only to feed others?
She considers her own
body of
fingers as if to say: What is
a mother except
hunger, gloved
in patience?
She sips, or just
sits with herself.
I suppose she does not care
if her web describes
the plane of light
over a gully—only that
it vibrates—and her
regrets, if any, fall
like crumpled cans
to the floor.
She wants me to come in
or move along.
I replace her roof
and go away humming
a murderer's
song, for who am I
to judge a home
built on the wild
angles of a leaning rattle
and sideways drum.

The Hooded Vulture

Alone in a dirt pen, the folds of his neck
tuck into a dusty, brown cape: a plume
from a pit. My dangerous whim. I was reckless
and wrote how wrapping me in wings, he consumed
my body; and in my lover, I flew. I'd say
I was clever but, really, this raptor I mistook
for seduction, possession, and rapture. I walked away,
thinking I got something for nothing at the zoo.
Years pass. My child's in bed. But my lover returns
to unveil my shame: a gown he fashioned of bones
and feathers undigested. He tightens the corset
and when I start to weep, he smiles and intones:
My bird, how did you think this would end
when everyone you love, you use in the end?

The Clock

At some point we should address
this pile of anger you're sitting on.
Laughing, I offer the analyst
the clock my father left me.
I can see in the glass
my expression is ugly.
First can we marvel at the silence
opening up in my palm?
At the gears and coils, greasy
and smelling of blood?
At this carelessness turned
to precision: I show up late,
he is gone, but the arms—
they display the accurate time.

Try closing your eyes and
visualizing a peaceful scene.
It's night. I am studying
a train's route. There's a smokestack
wending through the pines.
There's a red lantern swinging
from the caboose. The boulders seep
cold air. The way to jump aboard
is similar to how I stand
on this rock—unclear.
Nothing is illuminated.
Nothing gets near.

Sleep is so important.
Doctor, you are in the doorway
and we are hostages to this beginning.
His death is a wall I cannot clear.
I stay up nights and find
an egress in regression.

Give me something
that teaches me how to swallow
his dying. Maybe he'll show up
and say, Child, it's time.

✠

Blood Moon

I address you
from a copse
of trees that
is a black, spear-
raised mass
standing at
attention
inside me.
Your silence
is fine. I guard
it, in fact, so
nothing can
move in.

Moon

(Mid-Autumn Festival)

Above the mountain
the moon holds a rabbit

who sprawls inside its
warren. I sit on the roof

and zoom a lens until
the rabbit disintegrates

into flaking craters.
I understand the moon

is not the clotted bottom
of a bottle holding my

father who would've been
a year older today.

The moon is a light,
just as a bird is a flying

thing. But then, birds also
sing, and tonight I hold that

the moon is
a hole in the sky,

and this lack
around which

I circumnavigate
can be the bolt in a life.

Moon

(Winter Solstice)

The moonlight turns the trail
a DayGlo green on our hike home,
and to keep our son going,
my husband tells the tale of a poet
who found solace knowing that far away
his beloved brother gazed up
at the same moon. My son asks why.
My husband and I shrug. The poet
was likely drunk, but fair question: Why
must longing be indirect? So the messy
child inside each of us does not
run amok? We behold the moon
in the absence of touch, this O
through which the time-space continuum
folds, where memory grows secure
inside itself until a brutal truth
is obscured. We trek. The cirrus clouds stir
until they spill across the sky and, through
their scalloping tide, the moon becomes
the giant, glowing eye
of a dragon, I say;
an eagle, my husband says;
a fish, my son says, and I like
his answer best, as if we walk
deep in the calm of a river bed
while the fish fly overhead,
describing how
they close the distance.

Spring Festival

(Lunar New Year)

Mountain mist
and tall feather grass
part but I can't
see him yet
in the forest thaw—
he is the dark
time waiting around
the bend while above
macaques drop orange
peels from an arthritic
bough. When acacia leaves
beat their tiny hooves
the black dog appears.
Then, three.
My uncontrollable spring
growls, testing me.
I yell until he shuts
his purple gums
and slinks away
trailed by his hellish
siblings down the hill,
where they lie,
their heads resting
in the reptilian feet
of Formosan roots.
My winter goes back
to sleep.

Moon

(Spring Equinox)

The dark comes on
gently, in dips of
swallows. We had
forgotten our swimsuits,
collected rocks on the beach
and ate onigiri for dinner
outside a 7–11. When bats
dart out from temple
eaves, we head north-
west and drive the same
speed as egrets, their
black twig legs flung
behind them in ballet
extension. We climb
above the sea where
the pink eye of the moon
follows until we slip
into folds of mountain
passes. We see only a few
feet of road lit by our
headlights, but still we
make it home this way
in the dark.

‡

Bangkok Traffic

The cars line up in the night's waiting room,
and it's another hour before I get out of the car
and run up the overpass. Below me, headlights stream
and the smells of exhaust, Tiger Balm, and sulfuric fruit
rise up—just Bangkok heat and not, I insist,
an anatomic shift in the air,
but at the hospital, the windows are open
and cotton is stuffed in your nose and mouth.
You wear your blue and white checked shirt. Jeans.
Earlier today you furrowed your brows,
opened your eyes, and raised your hand
to shoo us away for making too much noise.
Of course you left ahead.
Maybe you jumped into a parallel lane
and as I sat on my hands you passed by,
a profile of cheekbone, a shiny forehead, ambivalent
to being seen. But a body is still a scene.
On the way back to the hotel, the cars slip by
easily. At the light, I watch the incense unfurl
before the Erawan shrine, its mirrors
and marigolds throwing off the shadows
of mammoth gray pylons. People come here
to pray, but all I have are statements, such as,
I was ferried in a river.
It split into channels of light.
You smelled of the sun.

Fugue State

When the monks chant on the first night,
the crystal lamps tremble, and a wind
blows through the hall. The next
morning the embassy clerk punches
holes in your father's passport in exchange
for the death certificate. That night
the temple dogs howl during the rounds
of chanting, and the white casket
on a pedestal with a lacquer tray of food
by his head rattles. On the third day,
you study the tide line of sediment inside
a bowl of soup and later walk three times
around the crematorium carrying his photo.
Children feed a giant boar at dusk as your cousin
instructs how to pour holy water on an old tree
in the parking lot. The next day, your chest
heaves up green gunk. The next morning,
you leave Thailand for America. Two weeks later,
you have liquid in both lungs. Pneumonia.
A satisfaction floods in: It killed him, too.
You are a proper and devoted daughter.
After another month, you feel
like you escaped a burning building except for
this morning in late summer when you run
along the clay towpath and a blue heron,
ankle deep in the canal's reeds,
stares indifferently as you choke on the air.

Evidence for God

is a billboard on I-71 from Cleveland
to Cincinnati, where I meet up with
old friends for a wedding. They don beards
and suits, and we pose in a photo booth
in boas and Elvis glasses. In the gauzy
candlelight, I overhear: "I'm not older,
I've just lost my edge," six degrees
of Tanya Donelly, and an argument over
the gig economy until it's the morning after.
Some friends leave before breakfast,
and I focus on the grass that furs
the highway median on the return
drive to Cleveland. The next day I will fly
to California to clear out my father's things.
The last time I saw him standing, his soles
squeaked on white composite floors
leading out of the mall towards the train.
In all this remembering, I fear the nebular
feeling, the obscuring of the canyons
of his face. But who says this aloud
at weddings? That night, I dream about
my friends, but their faces refuse to be
filled in. Evidence for God is a billboard
along the highway and maybe the memory
of human scale—his shoulder pressing
into me, long after he walked away—
and the mercy of so many bored hours
with friends with whom we race to recall
obscure songs instead of memorizing
faces coming together in the vanishing
point of a hall.

Graceland Cemetery

Chicago

On a summer's day I wind past
the wheat motifs carved
into tombs of nineteenth-century
bourgeois families as the grass
unrolls and paves over the
buried. Looking for Mies
van der Rohe, I pass a mulberry
and red oak, and, at Lake Willomere,
circle and check off the stones
of Burnham and Sullivan.
I like the tidy, rising placeholders
for souls. But then, the thing about
God being in the details:
I watched my father placed in a box,
someone called out directions
so his spirit would follow us
on the highway to the temple, and before
he was slid into a furnace,
his brother pulled up a chair
to speak with him. Buddhists cremate.
Do I prefer a grave's distance
between me and what I'm
getting at? Or—ash. I consult
the map, and Mies is somewhere under
the sugar maple. A breeze blows
and in polished black granite
it's him, in Helvetica, his
business card at my feet.
It's style, or whatever
the dead want in the end—
evanescence or the edge
of a stone in the grass.

The Storage Unit

In a California heat wave
I find a black widow
behind the shoeboxes
filled with my parents' sky blue
airmail letters from Thailand.
Her egg sac is torn and
the nymphets scatter
over our flotsam: mother's floral
blouses, brass arm cuffs,
astrology charts, father's
engineering compass,
tax records and birthday cards.
For five dollars I gain access
to a landfill and fling boxes
into hills of printers and broken
shelves, but when I go to the beach
the tide wrenches the pillowcase
carrying his ashes from my grip
and shriveled marigolds fall
with shards of bone.
Devastation is slow
until quick, a foundation
sliding from a cliff. He was
the four walls
around mom's kitchen.
A wave reaches up
and drenches my shirt.
He'd laugh about the black widow
guarding our things
and tell me to get out
before the tide
knocks me like dice
against the high walls
of this coast.

cool season

Hong Kong Triptych

I. Birds and Taxis

A white cockatoo swoops through
the pink and blue buildings
and disappears into the laurel by the temple.
The red taxis disappear into the highways.
Nights do not bookend days; everything
diffuses into hours—light eating dark eating
light. The heart pumps on or drains out,
and birds and cars
disappear into other parts.

II. Laughing Thrush

From the metal rail
along the path overlooking
the harbor, he mimics the sounds
floating up from below,
for instance the sidewalks
opening up and swallowing
people whole.
A noisy fellow but sometimes
there's a cheeky bit
where in place of words
missing from school
books he is the silence
of the native watching
those who exit.
I haven't seen his kind
in a cage so maybe he keeps
to the underbrush
and carves away in the style
of water knifing
as it tumbles down the hill.

III. Star Ferry

I took the ferry home.
The moon was bright
on the harbor and
in the tilt of the boat
on the silken black water
I was already gone.

The Room in Palermo

The butcher wheels his cart dripping
with tripe past the stink-eyed cats
on the stoop and under a rainbow
umbrella a beefy man in a gold chain
necklace sells salted slices of *cucuzza longa*
over ice and we stop and eat and walk
and eat and find an empty dozing
street of green awnings like stacked
rows of bruised and half-lowered
eyelids. You follow me up
the narrow staircase to the apartment
with the warped shutters that let in
slivers of light that shatter the room
and we walk through their shards and lay down
our things and when you step over here
you step over the cracked tile the color
of dried blood and I joke about gelato
and ruins but when finally you get here
to me to the bed I remember
the light lifting from your collar
and the roofless church where the sumac
grew and I hold you in this place
I haven't yet turned
into dying love.

Yangtze Gorge

From the sampan
I see orange and gray
monkeys on a pebbled beach
contemplating us
while up on a crag
men flanked
by sparse trees
gather around
the steam from
a slaughtered pig.
They are submerged
now in the flooded
valley of our years
of marriage but
still I see the monkey
and the pig as formed
by that place
as opposed to bodies
composed in a painting
like we were that first year
of marriage. Sometimes
in the night in the bathroom
I stood and sensed everything was thin,
the walls, the mirror, fine
as a needle point drawing
holding us together and I prayed
to be changed by it.

Magic

On the roof deck tucked between
quivering palms it comes back to her
the word *love* overheard
in a dream sometime
with Mars and Venus in the sky
something something love a voice
said. She squints at roof tiles,
tries to conjure exactly what
Everything is . . . All is . . . vanished.
The problem with looking is
remembering the way
in. *Love is . . . in? Of?*
No, it is the night of sangeet.
There are drum beats.
An uncle in a gray silk kurta
punches the air then shimmies
and cousins thrust their chests upward.
They undulate, arms upraised
What is love? the song transmits.
Through smoke the groomsmen kiss
and time suspends or are they
rhythm . . . *Baby, don't hurt me* and
they pantomime, eyes closed: *No more.*
Aunties collapse on dining chairs in flounces
of ice blue and topaz silk and furiously fan
their necks bared as in the bravura
portraits of heirs and they *are* heirs
to something. On the way back
to the city, cobbles hard on the feet,
All love is . . . a pomegranate tree
next to a bridge in midsummer.
The fruit she reaches for, almost
ripe. She is falling or still asleep when
the words surface
(though not who said them):
You will have love. The voice is
everywhere.

Daydream in Luchon

4 a.m. my soul goes
for a walk in the rain
slapping gravel in the courtyard
under soughing trees in orange
streetlight until before me the lake
is capped in fog, and long white strands
of waterfall stream down
the inside of this green aerie
in the ultimate romance
of privacy. It needs, though,
mystery, a menacing drone
from a ramshackle barn, a wing
brushing by, an eeriness
at the far edge of a field where play
meets loss and now it feels
like a door is ajar—.
But back under the pendant
over the kitchen table, a fly
bothers a curled magazine corner,
gray lightens, there are sighs
from the bedroom, then boy
and man appear and I have
witnesses again. Coffee, salt, butter,
baguette, and peach juice
bring me back to primary colors.
I smell the light and taste the alarm
of marooning myself on an island
I created. I check the weather
and my vision clears up though
when we head out of the gates
I spy the Queen Anne's lace
and purple grass which disrupt
clean lines and reseed
themselves in the cracks
where made-up countries
lie in wait.

The Source

She throws tissues from her chair
when she is upset. Bougainvilleas poke through
the gates, brush my head on the way
to the train. I go up and down steps
in the wetness of June near the equator to see her and then
leave again. I take the red-eye to the other side
of the world where the sky is thrown open
into long, summer light.
The gravel glitters in a courtyard and
a grand magnolia offers two phosphorescent
blossoms—formal but not foreboding. I still
hold my breath standing before it
as when I carried mother to her bed.
I keep moving and take the train
to the original land of nostalgia, a condition
where mercenaries far from home sat and wept,
missing these mountains. The sound of cowbells
sent them over the edge.
Under the lake, clouds of white
threaten to curdle into ice.
Here I feel a weight on my chest.
I drive south, where the water
spreads dark and cool at the foot of houses
with terracotta roofs. An old magnolia grows here, too,
but in a lemon grove, earthly and almost mundane
in its view of street parking.
In the village I walk up the trail
to the source of Fiumelatte,
the shortest river in the world.
Up the crumbling steps I climb and imagine
what it was like to see my mother
at the beginning. To grasp her before
I grasped at the countenance of trees.
Our future history still there
to be emptied out. To unknot
whatever clenches my chest. That is,
to remember and forget.

Starling

in the kitchen the blue flame
   ignites under a kettle
out the window a starling
   shelters from morning
drizzle under fig leaves
   did the moon keep him up too
did it draw him in
as it drew water back
   to the shore to rewet and
press into the marks it had
   known before
while in bed sleepless
   I waited again for the feature
to begin begged for the waiting
   to end but in nearing
forgot why I wanted morning
   to come
I reach for the spoon
   when the starling wings
his acid-specked mantle
   to another room
now the space where it had
   clung bounces as in
the moment after
   meeting oblivion
I stir the milk into tea and
   am folded back
into the succession of
   mornings such as these
when I am delivered
   by a bird, free to be
haunted
   and free to leave

Everything Has Its Truth

a vaulted ceiling wants to keep leaping
the boys' cheeks are tacky with sunscreen
an explosion billions of years ago
keeps exploding in us
eggs bubble up on cast iron
lentils grit the pot water
did you eat lunch
tomato seeds slip between fingers
I hear we're a process
eat, please
voices from the TV
I must protect him from me
a gentle pat on the arm
mom is just thinking
being a good daughter or a good mother
is a bum deal
the waistband digs into the belly
a boy in the pool says life is short
but also the longest thing you'll ever experience
I'll quit when this pack runs out

Nettles and Elk

We straddle charred pines
and land in
  the nettles where
the hypodermic shot in
the calf feels
  personal. A wildfire
last summer strewed
giant pick-up sticks
over the trail. We see
  a lone moose on
the facing hill and
then a herd
  of wild elk, who
freeze. Their hinds then
trigger, and they scatter
over the hill.
  At the summit
we spill all our water and
run out of provisions.
On the way
  down, we lose
the trail. We both fall.
Our falling sounds
like elk stamping—
deep, rich thumps
  to the chest.
My feet sink into cold,
soft ground near the
Indian paintbrush.
  Our stumbling turns
into a falling away
from our men and
children and suddenly,
  we are lost, as we were
in our twenties and thirties
unable to navigate

lovers or family, and often
we took on the dented
shape of the grass bed
after the elk
 had risen in an
exhale. You say
we should hurry, so we
run, gulping air like
the fire that uncreated
 this forest, and we
disappear to each other
with only the brittle
snaps of twigs and our
 own panting as
company, until a faint slash
of road appears below us.
I sit on a log and with
 every cell drink
the light pouring into
surfaces. You search
the road and say
how far we drifted.

Pierrot le Fou

> Do you know how to tell your day?
> —JEAN-LUC GODARD

Outside is cool and gray.
Your birthday always falls near the equinox.
At lunch I watch *Pierrot le Fou* and follow the back of Anna Karina's head.
The dubbing goes out and there is blunt silence in a record store.
Later, I speak with mom, the screen freezes but then her eyes move.
She wants to leave the home.
The sun comes out, and I carry a scarf but never put it on.
I cook rice on the stovetop and want to speak with you
but kids come to the door asking to play with my son.
The smell of spices and chicken
warm the kitchen. No time to sit and ruminate
but that scared you anyway. My husband, son, and I eat dinner
and talk about our day but none of this comes up.
I want to ask you: Is this what life is?
Over ice cream you once told me to stop thinking so much.
In the movie Marianne and Ferdinand scheme, steal, then flee gas stations.
The ruffles of her pink dress disappear into the red car.
There's a picture of you standing next to mom
and she wears a similar homemade dress.
Godard was obsessed with American cars
and he made a movie about the breakdown of his and Karina's love affair.
Somehow that is the closest I get to you today.

Planet in a House

This person is often found wandering the forest having lost his mind.
—VEDIC ASTROLOGICAL SIGNIFICATION

The ringed planet
gifts wisdom only after
forcing one to march the monkey trail
day and night and even then
I try to name things
I have known my entire life
but the words will not
express themselves.
In the mist's granular
air, I am brought back to what was
an accumulation of contourless
analog afternoons on a sandy mattress
where the fading light blued my skin
under the strokes of a fan spinning the question
what's wrong? What's wrong here?
Until one year my lodestar exploded
and in the thaw on the street
the dogwoods
of my childhood came back in waves
and the cherries blossomed
early, the smashed petals
smelling like kindergarten work tables.
I saw wind and light spilling from each other.
I needed a moment to pull over.
There's a price to coming home—
a howl of how to strip oneself
of the self that wants a bird as it melts
into distance. How ash cannot be
wood again. How to be truly free
and not have to eat shit.
Daffodils find their confidence in bundles.
A woman talks to herself passing
the snowdrops under the Japanese maple.
Her footfalls measure the distance

between hope and disappearance.
I would like a room
to which she can return
and rest in its silent corners—
silences she knows
because she has lived there
for lifetimes churning aloofness into warmth
singing these are the children I found
and these words I collect
are the ones I return to
are hands slipping around each other
in the sink
as the sun pinks the curb.
I find a place for all of them
in the house I birthed.

Novice

A symphony of snores in the women's dorm
    met me when I came back from the shower at night.
I brought a camera and photographed angel's trumpets
    on that mountain in Chiang Mai.
It was not a cult but it was cultish. My father
    wanted to join the monkhood
and this was practice. I did not shave my head
    or wear robes though everyone wore white.
We meditated, listened to lectures
    and fasted. I was 23 and thought a lot about sex.
One man admitted he had had a breakdown and
    spoke with brittleness. A kind woman saved me a tray
of food each morning, because I fell asleep only
    as day broke and missed breakfast. After two weeks
I gave in and finally slept. Then I felt the bliss
    sieve out as we drove down the mountain.
My father and I were quiet in the season
    when monks air their grievances.
On the old highway lined with rubber trees
    we tried to see past the window
each of us invented. It's funny how
    the Way is pitted against the family unit.
What were we in that moment?
    Breathing becomes the kin
to one's aloneness. When we got to the airport
    he held an umbrella over us
during the afternoon rain
    and when the water began to rise
over the toes, I watched him
    disown his feet and decide to remain.

notes

"*Vassa* Season": *Vassa* means "rain" in Pali and refers to the annual retreat observed by Theravada Buddhists. It lasts for three lunar months, usually from July to October, during the wet season. The entire wet season lasts six months.

"Violent Femmes" refers to an alternative rock band. The poem is written in memory of Sarah Hughes.

"Leaving Song" is written in memory of Jessica El Bechir.

"The Forestry Minister's House": The last line grew out of a usage for the word "uncanny," or *unheimlich* (literally translated "unhomely") in German, found in Freud's paper *The Uncanny:* ". . . [this family] are like a buried spring or a dried-up pond. One cannot walk over it without always having the feeling that water might come up there again."

"Doldrums" refers to a video clip of the wandering albatross from the 1998 BBC documentary by David Attenborough called "The Life of Birds."

"She's a Maniac" refers to the song "Maniac" written by Dennis Matkosky and performed by Michael Sembello and featured in the movie *Flashdance* (1983). I borrow from the line "When the dancer becomes the dance." It was my intention to evoke the sensibility of Yeats's line from "Among School Children": "How can we know the dancer from the dance?" It's unconfirmed whether Matkosky meant to do the same, but the energy is there.

"Moon (Winter Solstice)" mentions a mid-autumn moon festival poem by Su Shi, a Song Dynasty (960–1279) poet. I was considering Su Shi's poem together with Carl Jung's observation, "Sentimentality is the superstructure covering brutality." Eugenio Montale also crept in: ". . . the things that close themselves in secure / circle like the day, and memory makes them grow / inside itself . . ."

"Evidence for God" mentions Tanya Donelly, a singer-songwriter-guitarist who played in the bands Throwing Muses, The Breeders, and Belly. The line "I'm not older, I've just lost my edge," is from Ben Brookshire.

"Graceland Cemetery" mentions Daniel Burnham and Louis Sullivan, who are architects. Ludwig Mies van der Rohe, a German-American architect, said "God is in the details."

"Magic" borrows lines from the song "What Is Love" by Haddaway.

"Daydream in Luchon" engages with a quote from *Crusoe's Daughter,* by Jane Gardam: "Do you find that much-traveled men are the most insular? Like Robinson Crusoe? If he hadn't got stuck on that island, Robinson Crusoe'd have got stuck on another of his own making." I borrow from the line "I adored the coffee. It meant primary colours to me. . . ."

"The Source" and "Starling": Reading Louise Bourgeois's *Deconstruction of the Father/Reconstruction of the Father: Writings and Interviews, 1923–1997* and Lewis Hyde's *Primer for Forgetting: Getting Past the Past* sort of midwifed the poems "The Source" and "Starling." Some ideas and language referenced from Hyde's work include: "Memory and oblivion, we call that imagination." "Every act of memory is also an act of forgetting . . ." I am indebted especially to Bourgeois's work and the way she describes the handling of memory in her art. I appreciate her characterization of insomnia as "the too-much-memory disease" and beauty as "only a mystified expression of our own emotion."

"Everything Has Its Truth" is a quote from *The Myth of Sisyphus,* by Albert Camus.

"Nettles and Elk" is written for Cecily Parks.

"Planet in a House" borrows language from Dogen, the thirteenth-century Japanese Buddhist priest: "Firewood becomes ash, and it does not become firewood again" (*The Essential Dogen: Writings of the Great Zen Master,* edited by Kazuaki Tanahashi and Peter Levitt, 2013).

www.ingramcontent.com/pod-product-compliance
Lightning Source LLC
Chambersburg PA
CBHW030122240425
25627CB00002B/58